Blue Ribbon PUP

BY CAROL KIM
ILLUSTRATED BY FELIA HANAKATA

JOLLY FiSH PRESS

Mendota Heights, Minnesota

Book design by Jake Nordby
Illustrations by Felia Hanakata

Published in the United States by Jolly Fish Press, an imprint of North Star Editions, Inc.

First Edition
First Printing, 2019

This is a work of fiction. Names, characters, places, and incidents are either the product of the author's imagination or are used fictitiously, and any resemblance to actual persons living or dead, business establishments, events, or locales is entirely coincidental.

Library of Congress Cataloging-in-Publication Data
Names: Kim, Carol, author. | Hanakata, Felia, illustrator.
Title: Blue ribbon pup / by Carol Kim ; illustrated by Felia Hanakata.
Description: First edition. | Mendota Heights, MN : Published in the United States by Jolly Fish Press, an imprint of North Star, Inc., 2020. | Series: Doggie Daycare | Summary: "Shawn and Kat Choi need to find a way to keep a bichon frise under control before their family forces them to close their Doggie day care business for good"— Provided by publisher.
Identifiers: LCCN 2019006810 (print) | LCCN 2019019200 (ebook) | ISBN 9781631633294 (ebook) | ISBN 9781631633287 (pbk.) | ISBN 9781631633270 (hardcover)
Subjects: | CYAC: Bichon frise—Fiction. | Dogs—Fiction. | Dog day care—Fiction. | Moneymaking projects—Fiction. | Brothers and sisters—Fiction. | Korean Americans—Fiction.
Classification: LCC PZ7.1.K554 (ebook) | LCC PZ7.1.K554 Bl 2019 (print) | DDC [Fic]—dc23
LC record available at https://lccn.loc.gov/2019006810

Jolly Fish Press
North Star Editions, Inc.
2297 Waters Drive
Mendota Heights, MN 55120
www.jollyfishpress.com

Printed in the United States of America

TABLE OF CONTENTS

fifi

Kat Choi had just finished placing pot stickers on a plate when her older brother, Shawn, popped one into this mouth.

"Shawn! That is for your mother's mah-jongg group!" his grandmother scolded.

"Sorry, Halmoni," Shawn said, grinning.

"Can we go to Mitchell and Sasha's house?" Kat asked their mother. "Your mah-jongg games are always so loud!"

"Actually," Mrs. Choi said, "I need you to watch Ms. Wu's dog."

"She's bringing her dog?" asked Shawn.

"Yes! Ever since it won a blue ribbon in a dog show, she brings it *everywhere* with her," Mrs. Choi said.

The doorbell rang, and Mr. Choi went to answer it.

"Arf! Arf! Arf! ARF! ARF! ARF! ARFARFARF" A high-pitched barking filled the house.

"Fifi! No!" a woman's voice cried.

A small, fluffy white blur raced into the kitchen. It tore around the kitchen island, jumped up on a chair, then leapt down and sat.

"That was quite a show!" Shawn laughed.

"Well, she *is* a show dog," said a woman standing in the doorway.

"I am Ms. Wu," she said. "I understand you two have a dog-sitting business."

"Yes," said Shawn. "Do you need someone to take care of Fifi?"

"Yes," Ms. Wu said with a sigh. "I have a business trip and cannot take Fifi with me."

"We would love to take care of Fifi," Kat said.

"She is a bichon frise, so she needs to be brushed every day and has a strict diet," Ms. Wu said.

"That's not a problem," Kat said.

Ms. Wu continued, "And she needs to be exercised inside so she does not get dirty."

"Uh, okay," said Shawn. "But what about . . . bathroom breaks?"

"The backyard is fine or a short walk on the sidewalk," Ms. Wu said.

"Sounds good," said Shawn.

Poor Fifi, thought Kat.

CHAPTER 2

Pampered Pooch

A week later, Shawn carried a huge, fluffy dog bed, two plush pillows, and four blankets into their guest room.

Ms. Wu followed, carrying Fifi.

"This is Fifi's room," said Shawn.

"It is very nice," Ms. Wu said. "And someone will sleep in here with Fifi?"

"Uh . . . sure," Shawn said.

Ms. Wu smiled. "Great!" she said, hugging the dog tight. "Goodbye, princess!"

Once Ms. Wu left, Kat said to Shawn, "Have fun at your slumber party with Fifi."

Shawn sighed. "I have the feeling this could be a long week."

The next day, Shawn handed Kat a pink brush. "Time for grooming," he said.

An hour later, Kat flopped onto her back. "That took longer than one of Halmoni's hair appointments!" she moaned.

"Well, now it is exercise time. Come on, Fifi!" Shawn called, running up the stairs.

"Arf! Arf! Arf! Arf!" Fifi barked, chasing him.

The children ran through the house, Fifi close behind.

"Let's go, Fifi!" Kat cried on the way back downstairs.

Finally, the children stopped, laughing and panting.

But not Fifi.

"Aieee!" Halmoni cried, tripping over Fifi as the dog raced through the kitchen.

"Either this dog behaves, or I am moving out!" Halmoni grumbled.

The next day, Kat and Shawn went to the library while Fifi slept.

"I hope we can find some good information," Kat said to Shawn. "Last night, I heard Halmoni talking to Mom and Dad about Fifi's 'energy.' "

Shawn nodded in agreement. "Before he left for work this morning, Dad said we may have to stop our Doggie Daycare business if we cannot get her to behave."

"What are you researching today?" Mr. Perez asked when Shawn and Kat arrived at the library.

"We were going to use the computer to look up bichon frises," Shawn said.

"You know where to go, then," the librarian said.

"Bichons used to be popular with royalty," Shawn read. Then he laughed.

"And as circus performers! It also says they are really athletic."

Kat nodded in agreement. "Bichons are misunderstood because they look like toys," she read from her own screen. "Hey, it also says they are great at agility sports."

"Agility sports?" Shawn asked, distracted.

"You know, obstacle courses for dogs," she said. "They jump through hoops, run up and down ramps, through tunnels—that sort of thing.

That's what Sasha and Mitchell do with their dog, Bouncer!"

"Maybe that's what Fifi needs," Shawn said.

CHAPTER 3

Problem Princess

When Shawn and Kat returned home, Fifi came running.

"Arf! Arf! Arf! ARF! ARF! ARF!" she barked.

"This dog has not stopped barking since you left," Halmoni said, covering her ears with her hands.

"But she was sleeping!" Shawn said.

"Well, she woke up," Halmoni said.

"She ran all over the place and even started chewing on the furniture!"

Shawn gulped. "Come on, Fifi," he said. "Time for grooming." He walked to the bathroom, then stopped.

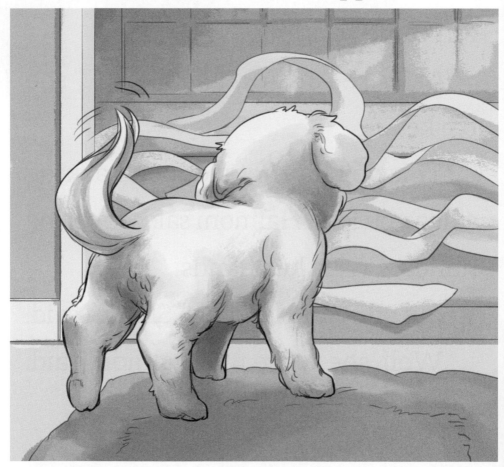

The floor was covered in little bits of white, fluffy paper. Toilet paper lay in ribbons.

Fifi cocked her head, tail wagging wildly.

"It's not funny, Fifi," Shawn said.

Fifi darted away, then began racing around the room.

"Fifi! No! Stop!" Shawn cried.

Crash!

Kat ran into the kitchen. "Not again!" she cried, looking at the pile of rice on the floor.

"That's it!" Halmoni yelled. "Out! Out! Out!"

"But Halmoni, Fifi is not allowed—" Shawn began.

Halmoni glared.

"Okay, we are going," Shawn said, scooping up the dog.

"Shawn!" Kat hissed to Shawn as he clipped on Fifi's leash. "She is supposed to stay in the house!"

"It is a short walk to Mitchell and Sasha's house," he said.

"Hi, guys!" Mitchell said when they arrived.

Sasha appeared, holding Bouncer, their Jack Russell terrier.

"We were just about to do some agility training in the backyard," Sasha said.

"Come see!" Mitchell said.

"Okay, but Fifi will have to stay inside," Shawn said. He tied Fifi's leash around the leg of the dining room table.

An obstacle course was set up in the backyard. Sasha set Bouncer down.

"Ready, Bouncer?" Mitchell asked. "Go!"

Mitchell ran beside Bouncer.

Bouncer jumped through hoops, ran up and down a ramp, weaved in and out of traffic cones, and trotted along a narrow beam.

"Arf! Arf! Arf! ARF! ARF! ARF! ARFARFARF!" Fifi barked wildly at the window.

CHAPTER 4

Agility Dog

"Poor Fifi," Kat said, hearing the dog's excited barking. "I think she wants to try."

"Maybe just one time," Shawn said, opening the door to bring her out. Once he unhooked her leash, Fifi shot outside, running up to Bouncer.

"Aww, they like each other," Sasha said, watching the dogs play.

"Here, Bouncer!" Mitchell yelled. "Show Fifi your agility skills!"

Bouncer ran up to Mitchell, Fifi close behind. "Okay, Bouncer. Go!"

Mitchell and Bouncer took off, running full speed.

"Do you want to try too?" Shawn asked Fifi.

Fifi barked.

"Then follow me!" Shawn cried and then led Fifi through the course. The dog's ears flew behind her as she raced after Bouncer.

When they were done, both dogs collapsed in a heap.

"You could build an agility course in your yard," Mitchell said. "It does not take much."

Shawn looked at Kat. "It is worth a shot," he said.

While Kat groomed Fifi the next day, Shawn, Mitchell, and Sasha set up a course in their backyard.

"Okay, Fifi, you ready?" Kat asked, opening the door to the backyard.

Fifi ran outside, tail wagging.

"Up the ramp, Fifi!" Mitchell said, running beside the dog. "Okay, jump! Jump again! Now through the tunnel!"

The kids continued to coach Fifi as she ran, jumped, climbed, and flew.

Later, the four children watched TV while Kat tried to brush out Fifi's no-longer-perfect fur.

"I'm not sure Fifi is cut out for pageant life," Shawn said.

"Yeah," Kat said. "Except Ms. Wu may have other ideas."

The next day, Fifi whined to be let out into the backyard.

"Okay, Fifi," Shawn said, opening the door. "Let's go!"

Shawn led Fifi through the agility course.

When they were done, Kat tossed Fifi a treat. "Good girl, Fifi," she said.

"Did you notice how much calmer she was last night?" Shawn asked Kat.

"Yeah. I think this exercise is making her happy," Kat said.

"I even saw Halmoni petting her when she thought no one was looking," Shawn said.

Fifi finished her treat and trotted over to them, her fur damp and muddy.

Kat gasped. "The yard is wet! Dad must have just watered it."

"Oh no! She is soaked," Shawn said.

Kat started laughing. "She looks so funny!"

"This is no time for laughing! Ms. Wu is supposed to pick her up this afternoon!" Shawn cried.

CHAPTER 5

Blue Ribbon Pup

An hour later, Kat sighed and put down Fifi's brush. "That is the best I can do," she said. "Not exactly show dog quality."

"At least Fifi is happy," Shawn said, watching the dog's tail wag back and forth.

The doorbell rang.

"Shawn! Kat! Ms. Wu is here!" their grandmother called.

"Hello, kids," Ms. Wu said. "And hello, my precious sugarplum!"

Ms. Wu paused. "What happened to her fur?" she asked.

"Uh, well, she got a little wet," Shawn said.

Ms. Wu's lips pressed together. "She was playing *outside*?" she asked.

"We are sorry, Ms. Wu!" Kat said. "But . . ." She looked at her brother. "Can we show you something?"

Ms. Wu's eyes narrowed, but she nodded.

They led the way to the backyard.

Shawn carried the dog to the start of the agility course.

Ms. Wu folded her arms in front of her.

"Ready, Fifi?" Shawn asked. "Go!"

Shawn ran beside Fifi to lead her through the course. Fifi bounded down the ramp, jumped over a hurdle and through a hoop, zigzagged around flowerpots, and flew through a tunnel.

Ms. Wu's eyes widened.

After three more runs through the course, Fifi came up to Ms. Wu, tail wagging.

"She really, really loves it," Kat said quietly.

Shawn nodded while trying to catch his breath. "And you know," he added,

"there are lots of agility competitions around here. We think Fifi is a natural."

Ms. Wu looked from the children to Fifi, panting happily at her feet.

"Maybe you are right," she said. "Plus, all that grooming was getting old."

"Just think," Shawn said, petting the dog, "with a new haircut, she will go even faster."

"Yay, Fifi!" Kat cheered. "You are definitely a blue ribbon pup!"

THINK ABOUT IT

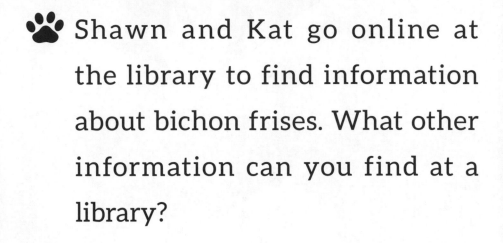

🐾 Shawn and Kat go online at the library to find information about bichon frises. What other information can you find at a library?

🐾 Ms. Wu wanted Fifi to stay indoors. Yet Shawn and Kat end up bringing Fifi to Mitchell and Sasha's house. Think about you would have done if you were in the same situation.

🐾 What, if anything, do you wish was different about this book's ending?

ABOUT THE AUTHOR

Carol Kim lives in Texas with her husband, two daughters, and one very well-behaved dog. Her childhood was spent in Southern California, where she grew up eating kimchi every day. She writes both fiction and nonfiction for children. When she's not writing, she enjoys reading, cooking, traveling, and exploring food from different cultures.

ABOUT THE ILLUSTRATOR

Felia Hanakata is an Indonesia-based illustrator. She went to the Academy of Art University and completed her BFA in illustration in spring 2017. She thinks storytelling breathes life and colors into the world. When she is not drawing, she usually reads, drinks lots of coffee, plays video games, or looks for inspiration in nature and her surroundings.